AN
EXTREME
TURKEY
DINNER

FROM THE
DARK MIND
OF

SEA CAUMMISAR

An Extreme Turkey Dinner

This is entirely a work of fiction, pulled out of my own imagination. All characters and events are not real (fictitious). If there are any
similarities to real persons, living or dead, it is purely coincidental.

If this story is similar to your Thanksgiving dinner, I apologize.
I promise that I made it all up. None of this is true.

CONTENTS

AN EXTREME TURKEY DINNER   1

KITCHEN CLEANUP   7

Bittersweet Memories   17

Preparations   24

Welcome   30

Toast   38

Tape Makes Everything Better   46

Friendly Laughter   51

The Real Toast   60

Cousin Phil   65

Improvising   71

Sister (Faith)   75

Cleanliness   is   Next   To   82
Godliness

Not A Hero   89

Getting   Better   at   Keeping   94
Hostages

Scott (Brother)   102

Poor Scott   111

Aunt Sheila   115
Uncle Joe   123
Poor Sheila   128
The Meal   135
The Main Course   140
Freddy   148
Forgotten Cousin Phil   156
One Year Later   161

KITCHEN CLEANUP

The light shone off the freshly wiped down countertops. Angie stared into the swirls of the marble as her mind got away from her. Even though she wasn't going through the mental checklist of everything that had to be done, she felt confident that today would go as planned. If not, she would be a failure, and that would not be unacceptable.

A quick shake of her head was all it took to focus in on the important to-do list. After a lifetime of trying to be perfect, even normal routine tasks seemed to be taxing. Angie's mind seemed to stay obsessed with how her entire life had recently changed.

The turkey was baking and most of the side dishes were already prepared. She stirred the gravy and even the swirling of the thin brown substance seemed to hypnotize her. Once again, she was lost in thought.

As her husband, Larry, walked into the kitchen, he pondered if it was too early in the day to grab a beer. He stood for a moment trying to get a feel for his wife's mood. After he was sure that she wouldn't chastise him for drinking before the guests arrived, he cracked open the top of the beer can.

Angie turned around, pulling away from the sweet memories her mind kept replaying. The look of disappointment on her face was obvious. Larry knew that he had to rectify his current situation. Preparing the Thanksgiving meal was hard enough on his wife. Him standing around drinking beer wouldn't help brighten her mood.

Larry took a long drink from the can and set it down. "Smells good in here, honey. Is there anything I can do to help?"

There were many things that he could *have* done to help, but that was in the past. Her husband had let Angie down many times, and the last major let down was the straw that broke the camel's back.

Angie remembered how life with Larry used to be carefree and happy. There was a time that she had loved him. That time wasn't in the present. For the past month, Angie spent most of her time living her mind. Remembering the good memories was where she wanted to remain. However, that didn't help functioning with the daily life she was being forced to live.

Since most of the food was finished, all she needed to do was to load the dishwasher. It would be an embarrassment if the family saw a messy kitchen. She was the perfect one, the one the family nominated to carry heavy loads of family stress on her shoulders. Angie didn't want to admit it, but she was at her breaking point.

After mustering up the realest fake smile that she could, she found it within herself to produce words. "Sure. If you don't mind, everything on the island needs to be run through the dishwasher."

Larry saw all the piled up pots, pans, and mixing dishes. Even though Thanksgiving dinner was a large meal, he didn't see why it required so many dirty dishes. Instead of drinking his beer, he had to help his wife prepare for the guests. He wished holidays would just be easier. Especially after everything they had been through.

As he opened the door on the dishwasher he nodded his head. "Honey." He paused, trying to find the correct verbage. "You don't think it's too soon? We can still cancel. It's only been a month."

Anger flashed in Angie's eyes. "Too soon? It's only been a month. That's why I feel the need to have the family over. I want them close to me."

Larry cleared his throat. "Right, but your sister offered..."

Angie grabbed the mixing bowl from her husband and loaded it into the dishwasher herself. "Stop right there! My sister offers too little, too late. I want MY family in MY home for MY holiday!"

Larry knew he shouldn't say anything. He even understood why she only invited her family this year. Usually, his family would join in the holiday happiness. Angie decided it would be best this year if it was just her family.

He wrapped his arms around his wife as she rinsed out a pot in the sink. "You know how much I love you right? The doctor even said it might be too soon. I just want to make your life the best I can."

Even though she recognized Larry's words as being sincere, she couldn't stand his arms being wrapped around her shoulders. Her mind told her to pull away from him, but she refrained from doing so.

She turned around instead and gave him a peck on his cheek. "Can you just load the dishwasher please? They'll be here soon."

Her husband hardly ever loaded the dishwasher. Of course, it was another thing he did wrong.

"No, Larry. The cups go on top. Bowls on the bottom shelf."

Larry raised both hands above his shoulders, making it clear that he wasn't touching anything in that moment. He was trying the best he could, still she wasn't happy with him.

Angie handed him a large butcher knife and a large double

prong cooking fork. "Okay, I know you've never done this before. These go in that little slot. Careful though, the metal tips point in the air. It gets more hot water on the dirty end."

She watched him load the sharp weapons just like she had instructed him to. Accidentally, she spilled water from the bowl she had been rinsing on the kitchen floor.

Larry knew how to clean up a wet puddle. He walked around the open door of the dishwasher and grabbed a rag. "Here, I'll wipe that up for you."

As Larry bent down to clean up the puddle, Angie used the heel of her foot and kicked him in the small of his back. Larry fell face forward, and tried to regain his balance by grabbing a hold of the counter. However, his hand didn't find anything to grab onto.

Angie just watched as Larry's face fell straight into the sharp knife and double pronged fork. She patted herself on the back for making him load the utensils into the dishwasher with the sharp points sticking in the air.

Larry slowly lifted his neck. The two tips of the large fork had struck him directly into his eyeball. The wooden handle looked like it was floating in the air.

The butcher knife had only scraped him across his cheek. He looked to his wife for help, but she didn't offer any. She just watched as the door of the dishwasher collected blood. The little spot where you put the soap was full of blood instead.

The only problem was that he wasn't dying. She wished him dead.

Angie's whole world seemed to be spinning in slow motion. Larry's hand reached for the wooden handle of the large double pronged fork.

Angie rushed to her husband's side. "Be still. Let me get that for you. I'm calling an ambulance right now."

She grabbed the fork and it made a suctioning noise as she pulled it loose from the liquid of his eyeball. However, she only thought it came loose from the eyeball. Even though the fork was no longer lodged into his head, Larry's eyeball was still attached to the two sharp prongs.

Angie didn't even bother removing the eyeball. Instead, she plunged it deep into the side of his neck, and she had never felt better in her life. Blood spurted out the side of his neck, staining her kitchen floor a crimson color.

Larry just groaned. Everything wasn't happening in slow motion for him. Everything seemed to be happening too fast. Perhaps he was in shock. He just used his one remaining eye to watch the blood pool up around him. Before he could even blink, his wife stabbed him repeatedly with the large fork.

Soon his body fell limp. Angie

kicked him to verify that he was dead. Larry didn't move.

She checked the time on her wrist. She still had a few minutes before her guests would arrive.

Instead of cleaning up the kitchen, she just shook her head in disgust. "Look at you Larry! Always making a mess of everything! You did this! You deserved this!"

Relief flooded her body. She had been working with a therapist about trying to forgive him. Now, there was no need for forgiveness. Revenge felt better.

She still had time to go upstairs and remove her bloody clothes. She wanted to look nice before her guests arrived.

It was Thanksgiving after all. She wanted everything to be perfect. Plus, she knew that perfection was always expected of her.

BITTER-SWEET MEMORIES

Angie climbed the sixteen steps to the upstairs of her home. As she reached the top, her head peeked around the corner to ensure that one particular door was shut. She refused to walk the hallway unless *that* door was shut.

Larry's blood on her skin was starting to feel sticky and she knew that she couldn't greet her guests with blood on her face. Not only did she have to change clothes, she even had to wash off all her make-up, and reapply all of it.

Luckily, she was perfect at everything she did, even time management. She would have more than enough time to make herself presentable. It didn't take but ninety seconds to use a make-up remover cloth and remove all her foundation. Then, approximately another ninety seconds to put her foundation back on.

Just for kicks, she added more bright red lipstick to her lips. As she glanced at herself in the mirror, her defined nose and red lips made her think of her mother in the picture from what she referred to 'the good ole days'.

Angie had received most of her facial features from her mother. Everything except for her dad's blue eyes that gave her a soft and kind look. However, even her hair color was the same color as her mother's hair was before it started turning gray.

She was inspecting her face in the mirror to ensure that all of Larry's blood was removed and she was satisfied with her appearance.

As she turned around to change into her freshly ironed black dress, a noise from the hallway grabbed her attention. Without even bothering to fully zip up the dress in the back, she *had* to check the hallway. The noise was a more pressing matter than whether or not her dress was or wasn't zipped up.

The woman slinked with the grace of a cat, careful not to make any noise as she walked softly on her tip-toes to the doorway. Once positioned in the doorway, Angie took a deep gulp.

At the microscopic speed of a turtle, her neck extended just beyond the door frame so she could peek down the hallway. Her mind had to know if that one door was closed.

Her eyes scanned the hall for any obvious signs of life, only to find nothing. Of course, *that* door was still closed. A tear formed in the corner of her eye, but she wanted to look perfect today. As always it was expected of her.

She denied the tear passage down her cheek. Her make-up was fresh and she refused to let any tear drops ruin her perfect day.

Since her own eyes had verified *that* door was still closed, she reached around and zipped up the rest of her dress. In the full-length mirror, the black dress hung perfectly on her body.

Of course, she ate healthy the majority of the time and would find a few minutes everyday to dedicate to the treadmill. It paid off in moments like these. Even though she acknowledged that she was getting older, at least she still looked good.

Angie dreaded the fact that she would be turning thirty-nine years old soon. But she didn't let that get her down. Most of her life had been a perfect one.

Of course, it was only perfect because Angie made it that way. Her mother had raised her in the era of when women didn't work. Her teen years were spent learning how to make a perfect bed and how to co-ordinate meals so that all the dishes were ready at the same exact time.

Therefore, for the most part, Angie had the perfect marriage. Her marriage was only perfect because she was the perfect wife. Larry was not the ideal husband, but he was always happy with her.

Her house stayed perfectly clean. It didn't matter if she had a million things on her to-do list. She would sacrifice sleep if that's what it meant to keep a perfect home. It's what was expected of her.

A newly formed wrinkle on Angie's forehead stuck out like a sore thumb compared to how young the rest of the skin on her face looked. She knew all those years of trying to be perfect finally caught up with her.

As she went back downstairs to check on the turkey, an open door in the hallway caught her eye. It wasn't the door that she feared to be open, but still it was a door that she didn't remember being open earlier.

Like a child playing a game, she barely stuck her head around the door frame to see inside the room. It was no surprise that the chair with wheels was still tucked away in the corner of the room.

The wheelchair hadn't moved in about a month. It's not like it was used everyday even when it was used. Only on the bad days. And the bad days were the worst.

Right smack in the center of the room, the hospital bed was the focal point. The floor creaked sending shivers up Angie's spine as she neared the large contraption. She didn't want to think about who that bed had been for.

Somehow, her mind was just as good at forgetting stuff as it was when it came to learning new stuff. Angie felt powerful in this moment, shutting out all the memories. She learned that she was also a perfect forgetter.

She could be perfect at anything that she wanted to.

Today was a big day, perhaps the biggest day of her life. Therefore, she used her perfect personality to perfectly shut down all emotions. Right now, in this moment, she didn't need emotions.

At least not yet. Memories would be needed soon, but not now.

Now, all that mattered was the plan. And she was determined that today her plan would be executed perfectly. After all, that was what her family always expected of her.

PREPAR-
ATIONS

Even though a film had started to form on top of the gravy, all of the food was going to be perfect. Angie stirred the gravy and cheated as she took a tiny sip of it from the spoon.

She knew that the cook shouldn't taste the food before the guests, but today she felt like breaking a few rules.

The turkey would be finished baking soon. Angie basted it with some more butter to keep it moist and delicious.

As she got the fine china out

of the cabinet, she tried to remember the last time that she had used the luxurious plates. Since she had a hard time remembering, that meant that it had been too long since she had entertained.

Entertaining guests was something that Angie always loved to do. It felt like years since her life had afforded her time to entertain. Since she had only ever worked inside of the home, cooking for a group of people was the most rewarding job that she could ever ask for.

Before life got complicated, her and Larry would have friends over at least once a month. Angie impressed all of Larry's colleagues with her baking skills and how she was always ready to please guests and keep her home clean.

Having guests over was usually the highlight of Angie's life. Even though she loved working inside of the home, it got boring sometimes. Now, in this moment, she wished it would have been possible to go back to her old boring life.

Larry's dead body lying in the middle of the kitchen floor was a reminder that it was too late for that. And in her own mind, she knew it had been too late before she killed Larry. Things just could never be the same ever again.

She pushed the old memories from her head. Memories that she told herself that she wouldn't let steal her focus today. She needed her focus today.

Her shaking hand removed the child-proof cap from the orange medicine bottle. After counting on her hand how many guests would be arriving today, she counted out two pills per adult guest, and only one pill per child.

She made sure to keep the piles separate.

Using a rolling pin, she placed the pills in a clear baggy and crushed them until they were nothing more than piles of powder. From experience, she knew this powder would dissolve easily in any liquid and could not be tasted.

Unfortunately, she had been forced to do this routine many times. But it was different in the past. In the past, she didn't want to have to do it. Today, she wanted to do it. Today, it made sense.

The fingers on her hand flinched as she tried to hold back her anger. Instead of just rolling the pills into dust, she realized that she was slamming the rolling pin hard into the marble countertop.

The wooden utensil bounced back in the air, threatening to smack her in her nose. She couldn't help but to laugh out loud. It was the first time she had laughed in over a month.

The laugh was not your everyday chuckle. This was a sound that resonated true happiness. The thought of her breaking her own nose tickled her belly. Laughing at herself was the best emotion she had felt in a long time.

After realizing how hard she was being on the pills, she slowly rolled the cylindrical object over them, making sure to crush them into fine flecks of powder. They had to dissolve quickly, and she couldn't chance anyone seeing crushed up pills.

With the wine being room temperature, it would help the medicine to disintegrate faster. Hopefully, none of her family members would suspect foul play.

There would be a child present, her nephew. She hated the thought of harming a child. Just a little something to help him sleep wouldn't be a bad thing. Soda would be the best way to get the poison in his system. She just hoped that it wouldn't be too much poison for his small bodied frame.

Now she had just enough time

to set the table and make it look perfect. As soon as the guests arrived she wanted them to feel comfortable with how she assigned their seating arrangements.

The turkey was huge and juicy and was the perfect centerpiece for Thanksgiving. Perfectly white doilies under each serving tray set the tone for a high-class meal. The fine china was laid out before each chair.

Angie even took the time to get the last little bit of smudge off the fine silverware.

The gracious host stepped back from the table and took a moment to take it all in. Everything looked perfect.

After already pouring everyone a glass of wine and making sure there was enough medicine in it to knock them out, she sat and waited. Soon. The guests would be here soon.

WELCOME

Angie was lost in her thoughts. Memories of past Thanksgivings flooded her fragile nervous system sending her back to a happier time in her life. A smile threatened to creep across her lips as she relived the past. But all of a sudden, the dinging of the doorbell required her full attention.

The real smile that almost crept up on her was soon replaced with the realest fake smile she could produce. It was the proper way for a gracious host to receive her guests.

Angie used both hands to flatten her black dress against her chest to ensure that there couldn't possibly be a wrinkle in the garment. A quick glance of her reflection in the china cabinet reassured her that every single hair was in its correct position.

With the fake smile plastered in its perfect position, Angie opened the front door. "Welcome Uncle Joe." Her eyes glanced down at him in the wheelchair but then quickly averted her glance upwards to the hands that were pushing his wheelchair. "Aunt Sheila, you look as great as ever. What's the secret? It's been at least a year, but you look as young as ever."

Even though Aunt Sheila loved compliments, she could spot a fake line when she heard one. She just pushed the wheelchair into the doorway, nearly knocking Angie to the side.

Uncle Joe turned up his hearing aid. Since he turned eighty years old his health was slowly declining. "It's cold out here. Can't we just come in?"

Angie jumped out of the way of the large wheels on the wheelchair to save her toes. As usual, her aunt and uncle were getting ruder in their old age. She should have known to be expecting them first. They prided themselves on the fact that they woke everyday at the crack of dawn.

They had even acted like a late-lunch Thanksgiving dinner would impose on their early sleeping scheduled routine. Today, it was important that her family be with her. Even her rude aunt and uncle.

After Aunt Sheila wheeled Uncle Joe to the dining room table, the doorbell rang once again. Angie was thrilled that she didn't have to make small talk with her elderly aunt and uncle. She had to be the perfect hostess, which meant she had to open the door for her new guests. It would be rude to leave them outside in the cold November weather.

A peek out the peephole let her know that her sister and husband were waiting outside. She couldn't see her nephew, because he was just a child and he was too short for the peephole. A chill ran along Angie's spine as she tried to force a welcoming smile on her face.

After gathering herself, Angie's lips spread wide and revealed her perfectly white teeth. As soon as she opened the door, her ten-year old nephew, Freddy, grabbed her around her knees and squeezed to give his favorite aunt a hug.

Since she had to be the perfect host, not only did she pat Freddy on his head, but she also hugged her sister to welcome her into the warm home. Her sister, Faith, handed the long coat she had been wearing to Angie to hang in another room.

Faith's good-looking husband, Mark, squeezed Angie's shoulder and asked her how she was doing. Instead of telling the truth, she lied and told him that she was well. Of course, that would be the answer a perfect host would give.

It was the look in Mark's eyes that upset Angie. It was a discerning glare that landed somewhere between pity and sympathy. Angie's mind couldn't decide which one would be worse, but she didn't want either one. She just wanted a nice meal with her family.

Freddy ran into the dining room. The thought of her young nephew being here today made her shudder. She wished he didn't have to be here for Thanksgiving, but she couldn't give a solid reason to ask her sister not to bring him. She actually loved Freddy.

The thought of him being here made her second guess her Thanksgiving dinner plans.

Faith was two years older than Angie, but looked much younger. Faith had a carefree attitude and seemed to never worry about anything. On the other hand, Angie was a worry wart that made sure everything was always perfect.

She left her guests to mingle in the dining room as she went and hung the coats in the hallway closet. She could hear them whispering. She knew they were talking about her behind her back, but she didn't mind. Angie was used to it.

After realizing that she hadn't asked her guests to not enter the kitchen, she raced back to the dining room. Luckily, everyone was still seated at their assigned seats. Angie knew it was sloppy leaving her dead husband lying in a pool of blood on the kitchen floor. But she was new to murdering people and wasn't prepared for how hard it would be to hide.

Nonchalantly, Angie slid a small table that was sitting in the corner of the dining room in front of the door that led to the kitchen. Now, she was sure that her guests wouldn't find Larry in a pool of blood in front of the dishwasher.

Once again, the doorbell rang. Her last guest had now arrived. She had been expecting her brother, Scott. She was actually shocked that he took the time to travel home for the holidays this year. Ever since his career as a photographer for a magazine took off he hadn't made it home for any holidays.

Actually, it had been three years since he had a Thanksgiving dinner with his family.

After seating him at the table with the rest of the guests, she thanked him for clearing his schedule, because this meal was very important to Angie. Naturally, he didn't want to miss his mother's funeral last month. At least now he was in town for the holidays.

Angie sat at the head of the table and was shocked that nobody even bothered to ask where her husband was. She wouldn't have told them the truth anyways. But she was lucky that none of them asked. Angie might be a lot of things, but a liar wasn't one of those things.

She could lie and tell them that she was fine when they asked how she was doing, but they saw right through her. On the few occasions that she did lie, she wasn't good at it. Whomever she was speaking to would always question her authenticity because her dishonesty was so obvious.

Now, everyone had arrived. It was time to start the activities.

Dining room seating arrangement

Angie (Head of table)

Uncle Joe	I	IFaith(sis)
Aunt Sheila	I	IMark(bro/law)
Scott (brother)	I	IFreddy(neph)

TOAST

The tears were threatening to leak from Angie's eyes as she looked at the empty seats. In a fair and not cruel world, there should have been two more guests for her Thanksgiving dinner, but the world had different plans. Evil glares at the empty seats wouldn't make the people she wanted to be seated in those seats appear.

Instead, Angie focused on the guests that were there. She was surrounded by family, and today she had special plans for them. In this moment, nothing was more important to her than making sure that her plans were followed perfectly. There was no room for error. In her whole entire life, there never seemed to be room for error.

However, even though she had done everything perfect in her life, it hadn't turned out how she had wanted it to.

She watched as her brother Scott teased with her young nephew Freddy about having a girlfriend. Kids seemed to be resilient and didn't bother with asking Scott why he had been absent for the past few years. Freddy just blushed and smiled like any child would. The rosiness of Freddy's small cheeks made Angie smile. He was innocent and pure.

That was more than she could say for the rest of her family.

The two empty seats that should have seated the guests that she wished were present weren't there. Their vacancy seemed to mock her. The world had a crazy way of reminding her of the state of despair her life was in.

Once again. Angie was sucked into the vortex of her mind. Past memories called to her, beckoning her to live her happy life of the past. It was the only way she knew to overlook her current situation. The memories of what used to be made her happy.

Faith, Angie's sister, called her name because she noticed that Angie was just staring at the half-empty table. It wasn't until Faith grabbed her hand that Angie found herself pulled back into reality.

Faith squeezed her sister's hand. "Angela. Thank you for inviting us. I don't know what I'm smelling, but that smell coming from the kitchen smells great."

Angie cringed at the mention of her birth given name. She hadn't been called Angela in a very long time. Instead of focusing on the fact that her sister didn't know that she hated the name Angela, she smiled.

The warmth of the smile radiated off the white of her teeth, making Faith feel welcome in her sister's home.

Internally, Angie laughed that the smell from the kitchen could have been Larry's rotten dead body. Fortunately, the smell of the turkey overpowered the smell of the iron of Larry's blood that puddled up on the kitchen floor.

Angie pondered how she would clean the soaked in blood from her hard wooden floors, but eventually realized that it didn't matter. She had other plans.

"I'd like to welcome each and every one of you." Angie held a finger in the air, signaling to her guests that she would soon return. She moved the small table that was blocking the kitchen door and made her way to the kitchen. A tray awaited her that had five glasses of champagne and a cup of soda for Freddy.

Being the perfect hostess, Angie balanced the tray on her hand and carried it into the dining room. She placed the poison-laced drinks in front of her guests, one at a time. A quick announcement to wait for her toast before they drank made her guests uneasy, but they listened anyway.

In her mind, Angie had prepared this toast many times. She had put a lot of thought into it and knew it was perfect.

"First of all, I'd like to thank each and every one of you for coming today." Angie began her toast. Even though she wasn't holding a drink, she mimicked the gesture of raising a drink to her lips.

Her guests followed her lead and took a drink.

"Years ago." Angie paused, remembering a better time in her life. "When me and Larry went horseback riding, he fell off, and he messed up his jaw. Everytime he chewed, it would make a popping noise."

Angie's guests looked at one another but took a drink even though they were confused.

"Then, a few years later, he got drunk. And fell down. He landed straight on his chin."

Angie's eyes looked at her guest's drinks, signaling them to take another drink. They did so, even though they didn't understand why she was making this speech.

"Anyways." Angie shook her head. "After that second fall, his jaw never made that clicking noise again. It was almost as if everything came full circle and had their own way of working things out."

Once again, her guests took another drink.

"So, you all know that this past month has been bad. But now, let's make it right. Things always seem to work themselves out."

Faith glanced at Mark and Scott. Aunt Sheila and Uncle Joe had already drank their entire glass of champagne. Faith, Mark, and Scott killed off their drinks even though they were bewildered. Freddy enjoyed his soda so much that it was gone rather quickly.

Angie applauded. She watched as they all tried to keep their eyes open. Sleepiness was overwhelming them, and she could see that the sleeping medicine was working on her family.

"Cheers." Angie smiled as she watched her guest's struggle to keep their eyes open.

As Mark's eyes started to close, his head nodded forward. He tried to stay awake and his head snapped back to an upright position. "I'm not feeling well."

Faith had a look of sheer terror in her eyes as she watched her son Freddy lay his head on the dining room table. "Freddy! Wake up! Angela, what's happening?"

Angie just laughed. She smiled and told her sister not to worry about anything and that everything was just working itself out. Faith didn't know what that meant. However, it wasn't like she could do anything about it. Faith's eyelids became heavy and she couldn't hold them open any longer.

All of Angie's guests were sleeping soundly and it was time for Angie to get busy. She had work to do.

TAPE MAKES EVERY-THING BETTER

Uncle Joe's head hung in front of his body in an awkward position. Aunt Sheila looked very peaceful as she slept. Mark was the loudest snorer of the bunch. Faith's and Freddy's faces laid face down on the table.

None of her guests looked comfortable and Angie knew that if she wanted to be the perfect hostess she should accommodate them. When she used to give her mother the very same medicine that she laced her drinks with, her mother would always sleep at least one full hour. One hour would be more than enough time to do what she had planned to do.

Watching the sleeping child Freddy was serene and peaceful. He reminded her of someone else. Someone else that was just too painful to think about right now. Angie used one of the cloth napkins to wipe the tears from her face.

Since Freddy was an innocent bystander, Angie took extra care as she handled his limp limbs. She taped both wrists together in front of his small body. But as a precaution, she still taped his boney elbows to the arms of the chair. Since lower body strength was usually greater, she used extra tape to secure his ankles to the legs of the chair.

She treated each adult guest to

the same exact treatment. However, she wrapped the rolls of tape multiple times around their arms and legs. She couldn't chance any of her guests breaking free of their bindings.

It was comical the way Uncle Joe's frail limbs were taped to the arms of his wheelchair. She wondered if she even needed to tape him up, considering the fact that he couldn't move around much anymore.

For that exact reason she had made sure to buy plenty of tape. She wasn't even really sure of what she was doing, so Angie made sure to use two different kinds of tape. One tape was wide and thicker. The second type of tape was more like a rubber material. She crossed her fingers that using lots of both different types of tape would be enough to restrain her guests.

Angie didn't use the same procedure on her other guests as she had on Freddy. Instead of being careful with their sleeping limbs, she twisted and contorted them however which way she felt was necessary to get the job done.

Once everyone's arms and legs were taped to the chairs, Angie could have kicked herself. The dining room chairs were made of wood and she hoped that she would have thought about that before covering them with the adhesive of the tape. With any luck, her chairs would not be ruined.

The last process of her plan was to cover her guest's mouths with the tape. She didn't need them to speak yet. If she wished to speak with them, she could always remove the burden from their faces.

The kitchen table was now a prison for all of her guests. She had control over them. They would be helpless to her. All of her qualms and whims would soon be resolved.

A faint laughter echoed down

the stairs. Angie jerked her head and looked upstairs, paranoid that there might be someone upstairs. There shouldn't have been anyone upstairs, but for a brief moment she wondered if she had been careless and forgot about anyone.

She was confident that there was nobody else in the house, but just to be sure she had to go and check it out. There was no room for error today. Everything had to be perfect.

FRIENDLY LAUGHTER

After ensuring that her guests would not be able to move once they woke up, Angie directed her attention towards the laughter that was coming from the upstairs of her home.

Whatever she was hearing sounded like someone was happy. Perhaps the noise was coming from a small child, but Angie knew that would be impossible.

In actuality, she knew that it was impossible for anyone else to be in her home. Each and every single one of her guests were present and accounted for, stuck to their assigned seats at the kitchen table.

Careful to not make any noise as she stepped, she climbed the steps very slowly and one at a time. She paused on each ledge of the steps and listened closely. She heard nothing but silence right now, but was positive that she had heard laughter just moments prior.

One of the steps creaked and filled the silence with a creepy noise. Angie almost jumped, thinking that maybe one of her guests had woken up until she realized it was just the age of the old home creaking of old age.

As she slinked up the stairs, there had been zero noise coming from the upper level of the home. As she got to the second floor, she peeked her head around the hallway, ensuring that everything was she left it.

The one door, the door to the

room she hadn't been in for the past month, was still closed. The thought of ever going back into that room filled her body with such dread that she could feel a raise in her blood pressure.

Angie's palms got sweaty and it felt like her heart was going to beat right out of her chest. A cold chill littered her arms with goosebumps. Then, she heard the noise again.

Her mind tried to make sense of what was happening, but there was no logic to explain why she was hearing a child's laughter coming from the vacant floor of her house. As badly as she wanted to ignore the sound, Angie knew that she couldn't afford to have overlooked another guest in her home.

Beyond the forbidden and shut door the faint laughter flowed out from beneath the small crack underneath the doorway.

Paralysis froze Angie's body, and even though she had tried to move, her body would not respond. Beads of sweat penetrated the skin of her brow moistening her face. Angie hated the emotional response her body succumbed to fear, but she was fearful that someone was in the closed off room.

Eventually, after standing still for a full two minutes, Angie's body once again gave her control over her own body. The room she had successfully avoided for the past month was beckoning her. Even though she didn't want to enter, she knew that she had to go inside.

As her hand grasped the doorknob, a jolt of static electricity pinched into her skin and she jerked her hand away. Even though she perceived it as a bad omen, Angie was determined to find the source of the laughter.

After taking a deep breath, her hand quickly stretched out and turned the doorknob clockwise. Even though her eyes were closed as the door swung open, she could sense a presence in the room.

It took a few times of willing her eyelids open, but eventually they opened, only to see a room with nobody in it. The door had not been open for a full month and it had been unchanged.

The pink bedspread was still wrinkled from where the bed had not been made since the last time its occupant woke. The closet door was ajar just enough for Angie to know there was no way that a person could be hiding in there. Pictures on the wall showed the smiling face of a happy child.

Angie's eyes began to leak tears that she couldn't fight back. The face of her daughter brought back painful memories. Each photograph seemed like an intrusion of her emotions. Sharp pains physically jabbed at her heart.

This room belonged to someone that was no longer around.

Even though she had forbidden herself from thinking about the hurt of losing her only child, she was overwhelmed with memories. She wished she had never stepped foot in this room.

It didn't take Angie long to figure out that hearing her daughter's laughter had only been her imagination giving her false hope.

Her daughter's unzipped backpack laid on the bed that was probably full of her school textbooks and what would have possibly been assigned homework.

As she grabbed her head to stop the painful memories, Angie lost her balance and had to sit down on the bed.

Her hand landed on the top of the backpack and she felt paper against her skin. Angie made a fist and her fingers grabbed onto what was labeled as 'ARTWORK'. The first drawing was of a pumpkin, the second of a turkey her daughter had made by tracing the outline of her hand.

Her daughter loved the holidays, especially Thanksgiving because even though she was only nine years old she titled herself as a foodie. Last Thanksgiving, Emily (her daughter), insisted on learning how to prepare the large meal with her mother.

Cooking the turkey was Emily's favorite part. She thought it was humorous that you stuffed food into the large, empty cavity of the large bird. Plus, each time they pulled it out of the oven to baste it with butter a savory aroma filled the room.

Emily was so innocent and should have had her whole life ahead of her. Fate had different plans.

Right after Emily's death, Larry forced Angie into a mental institution so they could monitor her. She was a 'suicide watch' patient because Larry feared she might kill herself.

The indescribable feeling of losing your only daughter at such a young age was a feeling that Angie couldn't describe to her doctors. Of course, they told her that grieving was the human response to death. But that wasn't enough to satisfy her.

No period of grief could ever help her forget her loss. Ever since Emily's death, her heart had a hollow feeling like there should be something that wasn't there. After spending days in bed crying and talking to several grief counselors and doctors, they eventually released her from the mental institution.

The doctors had told her that she had to stop blaming herself for her daughter's death. But deep down, Angie knew that she didn't blame herself for her daughter's death.

She did know who she did blame, but it wasn't herself. And

now it was time to teach them the error of their ways. That would be the only way to perfect her imperfect life.

Afterall, Angie had always been perfect with the perfect life. Why should now be any different?

THE REAL TOAST

Angie left her deceased daughter's room, knowing that she hadn't heard any noise coming from the room. But even with it only being her imagination, hope lingered within her that maybe one day soon she would see her daughter again.

She just laughed at herself and brushed the entire ordeal away from her mind. There were guests waiting for her, and she didn't want to be a poor hostess. She wanted to be the perfect hostess as usual. Especially for her Thanksgiving dinner.

After slinking her way back downstairs, Angie closed her eyes before she entered the dining room. She knew they would be upset with her, but she knew that she had to follow through with the plan. She silently gave herself a mental pep talk reassuring herself that she was doing what had to be done.

The dining room door swung open, and the first guest she noticed was Freddy. His tiny, young head still laid on the dining table in a deep sleep. Tiny slivers of drool leaked from the corner of his lips moistening the table cloth.

The other five adult guests were wide awake. Their eyes wide with terror, screaming through the gags of tape that burdened their mouths. There was only enough room for movement in their wrists, and their hands flopped around trying to struggle free.

Angie was proud of her amateur bondage technique. She now knew that her guests could not break free, no matter how hard they tried.

Aunt Sheila's wrinkles on her face multiplied as she tried to speak with the gag in her mouth. Uncle Joe, being the eldest of the group, wiggled the least. Her brother, sister, and brother-in-law, all flipped their hands as much as they could.

Even though Angie didn't know what they were saying, she assumed that they were asking for an explanation. Even though their perfect hostess hadn't expected to give them any explanation, she felt obliged to at this point.

Angie sat in the chair at the head of the table, and poised herself with perfect posture. She clinked a fork to her empty champagne glass to get everyone's attention. After shushing them, her guests stopped trying to scream through their gags.

"I would like to make another toast. The real toast. Let's say this is the official toast. I'm so glad each and every one of you could attend my Thanksgiving dinner. As you all know, this last month has been the worst month of my life." Angie paused to prevent any moisture from leaking out of her eyeballs.

"Each of you played your role in contributing to my grief." Angie pointed her thin finger at her guests in a circular motion around the table, but stopped as her aim landed on Freddy. "Well, almost all of you. Even though I am sorry that it has come to this, I'm sure each one of you weren't sorry for what you did to me."

Angie shook her head and her guests started to scream once again. She raised her voice to overspeak them. "All of you built me up to be some sort of perfect person my whole life. All that did was set me up for failure. Therefore, the blame falls on you. None of you cared when my shoulders got too weak to carry the heavy loads you forced upon me."

Angie paused to collect her thoughts. Seeing her guests tied up and finally getting the perfect time to exact her revenge was too much excitement for her. As she opened her mouth to speak again, the doorbell rang.

Angie wasn't expected anymore guests. Panic raced across her body, causing her palms to sweat. Her heart beat rapidly. She didn't know what to do.

Should she ignore whomever was at the door? Were her guests so loud that someone outside could hear them?

She knew she had to decide how to handle this situation, and she knew she had to decide quickly. Even though her perfect plan had been fouled, she knew that it was time to improvise.

COUSIN
PHIL

Since she had never held anyone hostage before, Angie didn't know what the protocol was for this moment. Thinking quickly, she picked up a butter knife and waved it in her guest's faces, warning them to be quiet. She even added the 'or else' to the end making it a threat.

She couldn't chance her guests drawing unwanted attention to the person standing on the other side of her front door. Then she laughed, knowing that using a butter knife was a comical way to threaten people.

Angie rushed to the front door, using both hands to smooth down any stray hairs that might have shifted out of place. Even though it was a brand new world for her to terrorize her family, she knew that she should look perfect while doing so.

Angie looked through the tiny peephole of the door, and saw her cousin Phil, standing outside shivering in the cool wind. At least he was holding a bottle of wine. Even though he was an uninvited guest, at least he was well-mannered and brought a gift for the hostess.

Angie didn't want her cousin involved in any of this. Over the years, he had actually been a very close friend. She couldn't have him involved in any of this.

Only her face could be seen in the few inches that she had opened the door. "Phil, what are you doing here?"

Phil, a tall man who hovered

above the hostess, looked down to flash a warm smile to Angie.

Phil's smile lingered even though he was obviously freezing. "It's Thanksgiving. Mom and Dad told me they were invited. I just assumed that meant I was too."

In that moment, Angie wanted to kick Aunt Sheila and Uncle Joe. She purposely didn't invite her cousin. Since she was improvising, Angie put on the best puzzled look she could muster.

"Whatever do you mean?" Angie started to shiver from the cold wind blowing into the crack of the door.

He pointed at the driveway behind him. "Mom and dad's car is here. Let me in, Ang. I'm freezing out here."

Before Angie had a chance to react, Phil placed his large hand on the door to push it all the way open. He handed her the bottle of wine and closed the door behind him.

"Phil. I'm a mess today." Angie tried to be honest with him. "It's best if you don't see me in the shape I'm in. That's why I didn't invite you."

Being the good cousin that he was, he just hugged her. Angie loved the feeling of his friendliness, but knew that she had to force him to leave. "Please, just come back another day."

Phil softly touched her face. "C'mon. I understand. But we're family. You're not getting rid of me that easy. You've been through a lot, I'm only sorry that it took me this long to visit."

Phil broke the hug and pulled away from his cousin. He turned to make his way to the dining room. Angie rushed in front of him, she tried to prevent him from opening the swinging door to the dining room, but he awkwardly walked around her.

He seemed to move in slow motion. He saw the tied up guests sitting around the dinner table, and his jaw dropped. He turned to look at Angie, but all he saw was the bottle of wine swinging towards his direction.

Angie swung the glass bottle as hard as she could. Even though the glass didn't break, it made a loud clunking noise as it collided with his forehead. He tried to throw his arms in the air to stop her from hitting him again, but he was dizzy and fighting for his own consciousness.

Angie swung the wine bottle three more times against his head until it broke, showering her carpet with red wine and a mixture of Phil's blood.

Shards of broken glass were sticking out of his forehead, looking like bloody jagged rocks protruding from his skull.

Phil fell to the floor.

Angie looked at her favorite cousin lying unconscious on the floor. It was too late to fix this error. Everything had to be perfect. She was past the point of no return.

IMPROVI-SING

Since Phil had never been one to push himself away from a dinner table, his large structure was hard for Angie to manage into a dining room chair. She tried lifting his body, but she couldn't. It was physically impossible for her.

And it wasn't helping things that the rest of her family was screaming through their gags. She just couldn't concentrate and figure out the best way to set cousin Phil at the table.

Tears leaked down Aunt Sheila's

face because she could see the large gaping wound in her son's head. Even though she wasn't a medical professional, it looked like he needed stitches. She wasn't quite sure, but it looked like the bone had even split in two. But she told herself that with any hope, that was just how the large amounts of blood had made it appear.

Since Angie couldn't get him into a chair, she took a different approach. While he still laid on the floor, she taped his wrists to two different legs of the table. The amount of tape she used on him was even more than she used on her other guests.

He had to be taped up properly. There was no room for error. If he were to regain consciousness, he could easily overpower her even in the sad physical state he was in.

It took her almost a full half hour to complete the process, but he eventually looked like a mummy with all the tape she used around his legs, taping them to each other. With the way both of his wrists were fastened to the table, he did not look like he was in a comfortable position.

Since he had always been kind to her, Angie ignored her other guests long enough to get a fresh wet towel and try to wipe the blood that had matted up in his hair. No matter how much blood she wiped away, more blood flowed from the large crevice.

She hadn't wanted to kill cousin Phil, and hoped that he wouldn't bleed to death. Plus, her carpets were now stained and she doubted she would ever be able to get them clean ever again.

Cousin Phil was just too nice for his own good showing up unexpectedly with a bottle of wine. However, she was forced to incapacitate him. It wasn't her fault. Everything had to be perfect today.

Angie thought to herself how the blame fell onto Phil. It was his own stupidity that caused him to show up at a dinner party unexpectedly.

Technically, that made him a party crasher, and party crashers weren't welcome at perfect Thanksgiving day parties. Therefore, she felt that she was obliged to knock him in his head.

SISTER
(FAITH)

Angie looked around at the guests that were vying for her attention. They squirmed the little amount they could in their chairs and screamed, even though whatever they were saying wasn't audible. Only sounds could be made through their gags of tape.

Her first order of business was her sister, Faith. After years of resentment building up, Angie would now have the opportunity to let her sister know how she felt about her.

As soon as Angie opened her

mouth to speak, her guests stopped making their sounds. She cocked her head sideways towards her sister. "I blame you for Emily not being here."

Faith shook her head in protest. Tears filled her eyes and mixed in with the sweat covering her face. "Hmm. Um Um."

"You know I can't understand a word you're saying." Angie leaned forward and used her fingernail to peel loose a corner of the tape covering her sister's mouth.

Angie peeled as much tape as she could, then placed two fingers around the loosening tape. When she yanked it as hard as she could, the tape made a sound as if it peeled some of the skin off her sister's face.

Even though Faith was now speaking, Angie wasn't listening. Instead, she was looking at the red, raw skin around Faith's lips. She wasn't for certain, but one of her lips were so red Angie thought that the tape must have cracked the thin skin causing it to bleed a little bit.

Since Angie wasn't listening, Faith spoke louder.

"Angie! Angie! Listen to me! Emily wasn't my fault! This is absurd! Look at what you're doing! Use your head."

That wasn't the response that Angie had planned in her head. In her mind she had replayed the same vision over and over repeatedly of her sister apologizing and asking for mercy. Now, Angie had her work cut out for her. She would have to force the response that she wanted from her sister.

Faith continued to scream as Angie left the room. She ignored Faith's words as she went to the bathroom. There was one particular item that she needed. In this moment, she was on a mission for that item.

After shuffling through the contents of the vanity, she finally found what she needed and carried it back into the dining room.

"Angie! Where's Larry? We're your family! Do you realize what you're doing? Larry, get down here! Angie's lost it! She's crazy!"

The mention of Larry's name made Angie laugh out loud. "You want Larry? I'll go get him."

Just as calm and cool and collected as she could be, Angie opened the kitchen door and saw her dead husband lying in a puddle of blood. His missing eyeball was a sight to see, and Angie laughed again. She grabbed a hold of him by his ankle, and drug him across the kitchen floor.

It was easy to slide his lifeless body across the hard wood floors. He didn't seem too heavy, until she glided him to the carpet of the dining room floor. When Faith saw his bloody body, she started to scream uncontrollably.

The rest of the guests followed suit and screamed out in terror through their gags of tape.

"There's Larry. Happy now? Now, Let's get back to you." Angie picked up the item she had retrieved from the bathroom.

She shushed her guests so she could speak. "You had the choice of taking mom. But no! Since I was the perfect one, she moved in with me! You didn't think about my family. Just your own! Look what your decision cost me."

Faith was in shock and staring at Larry's dead body. "I'm so sorry. Please Angie! Don't do this."

"I took care of mom! With no help from you! Have you ever had to cut someone's toenails?" Angie held up the fingernail clippers. "It's not fun. Here, I'll show you."

Whatever Faith was saying fell on deaf ears as Angie removed her sister's shoe. Luckily, her ankle was tied tightly to the leg of the chair so her sister couldn't kick her.

Angie grabbed her sister's large

toe. "This piggy went to the market!"

The blade of the fingernail clippers slid as deep as they could around Faith's toe nail. Before squeezing them close, Angie made sure they would not only squeeze into the hard toe nail, but also grab a piece of flesh.

Faith screamed out in pain. Since none of the other guests could see what Angie was doing, they could only sit and wonder what Angie was doing to her sister.

Angie grabbed the next toe on Faith's foot. A small stream of blood ran down between her toes making her laugh.

"This piggy had roast beef!"

Since the toe nail was much smaller, it was easier to jam to the thin blades deeper into the small crevice of flesh between the toenail and toe. Angie pinched the clippers together, biting off a piece of flesh.

Another line of blood trickled

down Faith's foot.

"Piggies might take forever. Let's jump to the other big pig!" Angie squeezed the other big toe on Faith's other foot.

Instead of clipping deep into her flesh, Angie bent her wrist sideways. The large toe made a faint snapping noise and Faith's toe was now bent sideways. Her large toe looked like a deformity.

It had been much easier to break than Angie had expected.

Faith screamed out in pain. "Please Ang! Stop!"

Angie just laughed at her sister. "See how hard it is to trim another person's toenails. And you put that burden on me with Mom. The responsibility fell on my shoulders! What I hated most was giving Mom baths. Did you ever give mom a bath?"

Angie stood and left the room. She needed more supplies.

CLEANLI-NESS IS NEXT TO GODLINESS

After removing the turkey from the oven, the perfect hostess used both hands to move it onto a large platter. After all, presentation meant everything to a good hostess.

However, what she wanted right now wasn't the turkey. Instead, she wanted the leftover liquified grease and butter mixture that the turkey had been baking in, Plus, she wanted it to be extra warm for her special guest.

So Angie poured the liquid into a large pot and added a flame underneath it on the stove top. After the liquid started boiling and pooping bubbles, then she knew that it was ready.

Using oven mitts, Angie carefully carried the large pot into the dining room. Faith was still begging with her sister, but Angie didn't listen to a single word that she said. She assumed she was mostly saying things like 'untie me' or 'let us go'. Angie refused to do either.

Angie looked solemnly at her sister. "Do you remember what you told me? That I was more apt to care for mom? Even though I disagreed, you gave me the pep talk about how perfect I was at doing everything. And you were sure that I could take care of Mom."

Faith tried to calm herself, knowing that her sister didn't listen to her when she screamed. "Angela. I'm so sorry. It's not too late. You could end this right now."

Angie shook her head no. "All those times that I put mom's care over my own daughter's care. Can you believe that? Now, you have a decision to make. Who's more important? You or Freddy?"

A look of terror invaded Faith's face. She looked at Freddy who was still sleeping. At least she hoped that he was sleeping. He hadn't moved in quite some time.

Angie reached into her pocket and unfolded the hand drawn turkey that Emily traced her own hand to draw. "I either nail this to his face. Or you're getting a bath. Your choice."

Faith looked confused. "Please, not my son. Do what you want to me, but don't hurt my son!"

Angie didn't want to ever hurt Freddy. Afterall, he was innocent in all of this. He had even been a good friend to Emily. She was glad with the choice her sister made.

Keeping the oven mitts on, Angie dipped her hands into the still bubbling grease/ butter mixture. "You do know that Mom liked her baths hot, right?"

Faith said nothing. She just sat completely still, paralyzed with fear, watching her crazed sister threaten her with the boiling grease.

Angie made a bowl with her hands the best she could with the oven mitts on, and threw the steaming grease onto Faith's face. Faith didn't know what was happening, she was too busy watching her sister that she didn't react.

Instead, the boiling butter juice speckled her face and tiny red blisters started forming. Faith cried out in pain as the grease invaded her eyeball. She tried to blink to wash the grease away, but it wasn't helping.

Faith tried to rub the grease off with her shoulder, but it didn't lessen the pain. Angie grabbed another handful of the substance and threw even more of it on her sister.

The muffled guests screamed in horror, knowing that it would soon be their turn.

Faith was screaming, begging for mercy. Angie ignored her. Instead she dipped the baster that looked like a large eye dropper into the steaming liquid. Faith was crying and begging and pleading as Angie shoved the baster into her sister's ear and squeezed it to release all the warm fluids.

Faith actually howled in pain, knowing that she couldn't take much more. The stinging and burning sensation down the entire side of her head was worse pain than childbirth. As the fluid oozed down her ear canal, she knew that her hearing was being damaged.

And even though the fluid had been poured on the inside of her ear, large red welts and blisters formed on the outside. The only thing Faith wanted was for her sister to stop hurting her.

Angie wasn't ready to stop. "I had to wash Mom's privates! Did you ever do that? Sometimes, when her diaper was full, it made a mess everywhere!"

Faith didn't hear a single word that her sister said, but the other guests did and knew what Angie was going to do next. Angie took the whole pot of boiling fluid and poured it into her sister's lap so that it would clean her sister's lap and bottom.

Faith howled in pain once again as she felt the hot liquid run along the curves of her sensitive places. She cried and begged her sister for mercy.

The boiling liquid grease rolled into all of her sensitive places. Her pants were wet with the liquid, making the stinging sensation even worse. Faith could feel the blisters form around her crotch. She passed

Sea Caummisar

out from the pain.

NOT A HERO

Mark, Angie's brother-in-law, couldn't stand seeing his wife being tortured. He wished the pain would have been inflicted on him, not Faith. All he could do was scream through his gag, even though Angie didn't care what he was trying to say through his taped up mouth.

He could also wiggle his wrists. Since he was right-handed, his right arm was much stronger than his left. He listened to Angie's words, and everything she said just made him madder and more determined to break out of his bindings.

He remembered a few years back when his mother-in-law had

been diagnosed with dementia. Naturally, Faith and Angela were devastated. Faith refused to take her mother in and care for her.

Faith said all along that their mother belonged in an old folks home where she would have twenty-four hour a day supervision. Mark knew that someone else in the family had convinced Angie that a nursing home would not be appropriate for her mother.

Angie wanted to split the caring for their mother. Her idea was to live with Angie through the week, and live with Faith on the weekends.

Faith and Mark refused. First of all, their social calendars were too full to worry about caring for her mom. Plus, they did not want Freddy to be exposed to dementia. Afterall, he was just a young boy and they didn't want the crazy old lady to scare him.

So after Angie refused a nursing home, Faith did tell her sister that she was perfect to care for their mom. Afterall, she didn't work outside of the home and their child Emily loved her grandmother very much.

That's how Angie became to be her elderly mother's caregiver. She felt like it was a burden that the family thrust solely onto her shoulders.

With each wiggle of his wrist, Mark was determined to get at least one hand free so he could try to untape his other hand. Then, he could easily overpower Angie and stop this day of pure chaos.

Finally Mark maneuvered his hand just enough so that he was getting somewhere. If he kept up the same amount of effort, soon his hand would be free.

Angie was laughing maniacally at her sister who passed out from all the pain. She pointed at her grease soaked lap and made silly remarks about how the grease couldn't be good for her woman parts. It could perhaps lead to an infection.

Noone else at the dinner table thought that was funny nor did they find it amusing.

Mark had just enough leadway to move his hand just a few inches to touch his wife's hand. He had worried that she was dead and not just unconscious. That's how he messed up.

Angie saw that his hand had a little bit of room for movement. She couldn't allow him to get free. After immediately stopping her jokes and poking fun at her sister, Angie frantically rushed to the garage.

She had to think fast. Once again, Angie reminded herself that even though she was new at torturing people, she had always been perfect at everything she had ever tried in life.

As a child, she was a perfect student and daughter. After getting married, she was the perfect wife. Then, when she had Emily, she was the perfect mother. Well, almost a perfect mother. If she had been the perfect mother, Emily would be here today.

So she had to think fast and improvise. After realizing that Mark was too strong for the tape around his wrists, she needed something stronger and more permanent.

She went into her husband's tool box and found a hammer. Nearby was a box of nails that Larry had used to mend a step on the back porch. Angie knew she could be a perfect torturer.

GETTING
BETTER AT
KEEPING
HOSTAGES

While Angie was gone, Mark could wiggle his hand more since she was not sitting near him. He could make larger movements and not be seen by his watchful hostess.

His hand was almost free. He kept nudging Faith, not getting a response from her. He feared she was dead, but he wasn't sure if boiling grease would really be enough to kill someone. He looked at his son who still hadn't woken up after whatever poison their hostess had slipped into their drinks.

He feared that Freddy might be dead, too.

There was light at the end of the tunnel. The tape was really giving away. He knew that his hand would soon be free. He was hopeful that soon he could help his family. He knew their lives depended on him breaking loose of his tape.

When the door to the dining room swung open, he knew that all hope was lost. Angie walked straight to Mark's chair. He didn't even see it coming as she raised the hammer over her head.

Since Angie never used tools, she even swung the hammer wrong. Instead of the ball point end falling down onto Mark's hand, it was met with the claw side of the hammer (the side meant to remove nails).

The two claws bit into his skin,

and it felt like his entire hand had exploded. The sharp end of the hammer pierced completely through his hand and snagged into the wooden arm of the chair. Blood splattered onto Mark's shirt and Angie's face.

Since she had already seen her husband lying in a pool of blood, this scene was not dramatic to her one bit. Most people would have been appalled or grossed out.

It just made Angie feel powerful. Now, she knew that she was good at keeping hostages.

Mark's hand was flayed and blood dripped onto her freshly cleaned carpet. She knew that after today, she would never get her carpets clean ever again. Chances were that she would have to buy new flooring instead of trying to wash all the blood away.

Even though she knew that Mark's hand was currently damaged, she knew that he would still have to be restrained. She grabbed the box of nails to finish his new bindings. However, he was screaming so loud that he started to annoy her.

Angie held the nail in the air, in a threatening manner. "Do you want this in your hand or your face? Because your mouth is on my last nerve. And I don't know if you noticed, my nerves are shot today."

Bewildered, Mark looked at his hostess. Angie was getting crazier by the minute. Now, he had zero hope for survival.

He tried to bite his tongue, he tried not to scream, but the pain was too much to bear. He couldn't help but to release noise through his mouth.

Angie got mad and she couldn't decide if she wanted to bust his teeth out with the hammer, or to drive a nail into his cheek.

For now, she just had to ignore his cries of pain. She focused on his hands for the moment. Even though he hadn't gotten his left hand free of the tape, she placed a nail on the top of his left hand.

She held the nail in place as she aimed the correct ball ping end of the hammer onto the head of the nail. She hated that she was ruining her nice dining room furniture, but she knew that she could always buy more furnishings.

It took four good swings with the hammer to drive the nail successfully through his hand and into the wooden arm of the chair.

Mark's eyes were popping out of his head as his screams just got louder.

She tried to lift his left wrist from the chair, but his arm didn't budge. She knew then that the nails would be enough to hold him in place.

After placing another nail into the split flesh of his damaged right hand, she hammered it through the muscles of his hand and into the other arm of the chair. She laughed as she watched Mark sweat and scream.

Still, he wouldn't shut up and she was very annoyed. She threatened him once again with the hammer. She felt like she was being fair to him, by giving him a chance to shut up and abide by her wishes. He just refused to be a good victim.

"You were always busy weren't you, Mark? You two were too busy and barely even visited Mom after she moved in here. What do you have to say about that?" Angie removed the tape from his mouth so he could now speak.

All Mark did was scream. He had been screaming so hard through his gag that his voice was raspy and hoarse.

Angie drew back the hammer, and Mark shut his mouth. Tears fell down both of Mark's cheeks. "Ang, I'm so sorry."

Angie stared into his desperate eyes. She knew that he was obviously lying. Mark was only telling her what she wanted to hear, but she was too smart for that.

"No. You're not." Angie brought the hammer down and it smacked Mark across his cheek.

Mark spit blood and teeth onto the empty plate in front of him.

"You never came to see Mom. I'm sure you're the one who stopped Faith from visiting her, too. So guess what? You'll never see anything again."

Mark screamed in horror, fearful of what was to come next. "No! Don't!"

Angie raised the hammer once again, and slammed the ball end of the metal into one of Mark's eyes. He once again screamed, louder than he had screamed all day.

Soft tissue dangled off the tip of the tool. Blood ran down Mark's face and it made him look like he was crying blood. The orbital bones of his face looked like they had collapsed into his eyeball.

Angie's shrill voice of laughter filled the room, giving off the creepiest feeling. All of the other guests cringed at the thought of what their fate might be.

SCOTT
(BROTHER)

Angie directed her attention to her brother. "Scott, you're even worse than Mark here. You were Mom's own flesh and blood. Still, you were never around. You moved states away to get away from our family."

Scott's thin frame trembled with fear. He had already known that he was a bad son and brother. However, he never knew that it would be the death of him.

"Would it be fair for you to lose both of your eyes?"

Scott moved his head from left to right as fast as he could, signaling no. He did not think it would be fair to lose his eyes. He didn't think that any of this was fair. Obviously, his sister was nuts and he knew that the mental institution had released her way too soon.

He had already hated himself for missing his mother's funeral a month prior. But it wasn't his fault that his job wouldn't give him leave. He thought coming home for Thanksgiving would make everything better.

Now, he wished he hadn't come home at all.

Scott either hadn't been as strong as Mark, or maybe his tape was thicker around his wrists. No matter how hard he tried to wiggle his wrists, his tape wasn't budging.

Plus, after seeing Mark get his hand nailed to the chair, he was glad that he hadn't successfully wiggled his hands free.

Angie walked around the table, in a dramatic manner with a wild look in her eyes. "You never came to see Mom. You never helped take care of her. You never even saw her on her bad days." Angie paused for a moment to collect her thoughts.

The blood splatter on Angie's face made her look like a monster. Something about her transformed as the day went on. Even her eyes appeared diabolical. Scott swore that he saw red lines in her pupils. Maybe she was possessed.

But no such luck. Angie was just a crazy lunatic hell bent on revenge.

"Some days, Mom didn't even know who I was. Did you know that?"

Scott shook his head unsure of the answer Angie wanted. He knew that she had taken on a heavy load when she was nominated to be their mother's caregiver, but he had no idea she would snap after everything that happened.

Angie was always the strong one. He thought for sure she would have handled everything better than she had.

After the accident, and Larry called him to tell him that Angie had been hospitalized, he couldn't believe it. It was out of character for Angie. She had always been so perfect.

Angie picked up a butter knife and a fork from the place setting in front of Scott. "You never saw Mom. It's fair if you never see again. Do you prefer knife or fork?"

Scott violently shook his head and tried to speak through the tape covering his mouth. He didn't prefer knife or fork. He wanted to walk away from this whole ordeal unscathed.

Slowly, using her fingernail, Angie peeled a small corner of tape from Scott's mouth. Then, in one super quick motion, she ripped it off his mouth, not caring if it ripped any skin from his face or lips.

Scott shrieked in pain and gasped for air as soon as his tape was removed. His lips had started to chap and crack. But that was the least of his worries.

All he cared about was trying to talk some sense into Angie.

"Angie. I am so sorry for everything. I wish I would have been a better brother, a better son. But I wasn't. But I'll change. I promise."

With the evil redness in her eyes, Angie just stared at her brother. He couldn't decide if she was believing his words or if she was doubting their sincerity. Even though he knew that in this very moment, his words rang one-hundred percent true.

He would actually say anything in this moment to save his eyeballs from being punctured with a fork. And actually mean it.

After her pause, Angie started once again with her shrill laughter that hurt her guests ears.

After knowing his words were unsuccessful, Mark tried again, but only with tears. He hoped she wouldn't notice that they were tears of fear instead of tears of truth and regret. "C'mon Angie. We're your family. We've always loved you. We still do. Let's stop this before anything goes any further."

Angie cocked her head sideways and stopped laughing. "Then butter knife it is."

Angie's cold, thin fingers wrapped around Scott's jawline as he tried to squirm his head away from her. She was determined to ruin Scott's eyesight. She hoped to blind him, take his job away from him. She wanted to be sure that he would never photograph anything in his life, never again.

The not-too-sharp serrated edge of the butter knife came closer to his eye. Even though he tried to squint, she wasn't deterred. Angie wedged the cold metal between his eyelids and started sawing on his eyeball.

The more he squirmed, the more pressure she forced upon the utensil. A mixture of a milky substance and blood ran down Scott's cheek.

The pain was a burning sensation not only in his eyeball, but in the entire side of his head. He opened his mouth to beg her to stop, but he couldn't produce any words. Instead, he just groaned in pain, feeling helpless about the entire situation.

Angie got aggravated that the butter knife wasn't sharper. She had been sawing into Scott's pupil for a full minute and realized there was still a snotty tissue that she hadn't even busted through yet.

After she threw down the butter knife, Angie rushed into the kitchen. A set of knives sitting in a butcher's block on the countertop called to her. First, she removed the butcher knife, but decided that it was too large and too long.

She decided on a smaller paring knife and rushed back into the dining room. Scott's ruined eye was staining his face with blood.

He was begging and pleading, but she deemed it to be too little too late. Instead, she honed in on the undamaged eye and took the sharp tip of the paring blade and dug it into the center of his eyeball.

The snotty tissue gave way to the blade, and a path was parted where the knife was buried in his eyeball. Even when Angie released the handle of the knife from her grip, the blade hung in place almost as if it was floating in the air.

Scott couldn't see her anymore, but he could hear his sister laughing at what she had just done. Then she asked him a question.

"Which finger do you use to shoot your pictures? Which finger is the most valuable?"

Scott trembled in fear and balled his fingers into a fist the best he could. He didn't want her cutting off his fingers.

POOR SCOTT

Angie tried to uncurl her brother's shaking fingers. He didn't answer her question, so she knew that she had to cut off all of his fingers.

Even though she couldn't unbundle his digits, she knew she could still damage his hands. She reached up to his head and pulled the paring knife from his eye. As it unsuctioned, it made a faint popping noise.

If she hadn't been listening closely, Angie wouldn't have heard it over Scott's screaming. But she heard it and it made her laugh.

It took some force for Angie to stab the small blade into the first knuckle, closest to the base of his hand, but she successfully forced the blade deep into his finger.

Once the blade was lodged into place, Angie jerked it sideways. More blood spilled onto her clean carpet, but she didn't mind. Scott hadn't been around in years and she knew that he deserved this.

The blade hit resistance and she wondered if she had struck bone. It took a lot of effort, but soon she slid the knife across the full base of his finger.

Even though it was detached, his finger laid upon the wooden arm of the dining room chair. Scott's screams annoyed her. But he was in shock, knowing that the pain in his eye would mean he was blind. And even though he couldn't see his finger, he knew it hurt worse than his eyes.

She plunged the knife into the side of his cheek.

The blade fully penetrated his mouth and she wondered if maybe she had even cut his tongue in the procedure. Once again, the knife was lodged into the hole of Scott's cheek and she had to remove it.

Just for good measure, when she pulled the blade out, she swiftly stabbed it into his other cheek. Blood was running down Scott's chin. Spittles of blood were staining her white table cloth as he screamed.

All she wanted was for him to shut up and stop screaming. She couldn't tolerate the unnecessary noise.

Angie plunged the blade into the soft skin of Scott's neck. The other family members looked at her in horror. Their eyes widened as they realized what their fate would be eventually. They then knew that

Angie had planned to kill them all.

Scott's flesh parted as Angie drug the blade upwards of his neck. She didn't pull the blade out until she hit the bone of Scott's chin.

Scott's neck opened up like a large cavity and blood poured from his wound like rain from a storm cloud. He only made what sounded like a few choking noises before his eyes rolled into the back of his head.

It didn't take long for Scott to die. Angie had officially killed her brother. She grinned at her achievement.

Even though she had been planning this dinner, she never knew for sure that she would have the gall to follow through with everything. Even Larry had been an easy kill. Her husband's death could have almost been assumed an accident.

There was no denying that her brother's death was deliberate.

AUNT
SHEILA

By now, all of the guests sat in silence. Maybe they were in disbelief of what was happening, or maybe they were just scared stiff. All Angie knew was that she was enjoying the silence.

Since she had been proud of what she had accomplished so far, Angie just smiled and looked around the dining room table. Aunt Sheila and Uncle Joe were the only guests who she hadn't gotten to yet. And Freddy. But she had special plans for her young nephew.

Angie smirked at her unscathed guests. "Aunt Sheila. My mother's sister. You and your big mouth."

Aunt Sheila just stared at her niece. She was in shock. Her mind just couldn't comprehend what was happening.

Angie began to mock her aunt. She changed the pitch of her voice to an annoying high-pitched one, and moved her head left and right as she spoke. "You can't put her in a home. Those places aren't fit for a dog. Nevertheless your mother."

Angie recalled that conversation like it was yesterday, even though it was a couple of years ago. "You even gave me Uncle Joe's old wheelchair! She had dementia. It's not like her legs were broken! But since you gave it to her, she chose to spend some days being pushed around! Were you here to push her around?"

Aunt Sheila hung her head in shame, regretting every word she had ever spoken about her sister. At this time, she chose to keep her mouth closed. It's not like she could speak anyways with the tape covering her mouth. Until Angie leaned over in front of her face, and ripped the tape free from Sheila's mouth.

Sheila just took an extra deep inhale, thankful to be tasting fresh air through her mouth. Even still, she sat in silence since Angie told her that she had a big mouth. Sheila did not like where this conversation was heading.

Angie waited for a response, but she didn't get one. She just strummed her fingers on the table, making it obviously known that she wanted to hear what her aunt had to say. "Well. What do you have to say for yourself?"

Sheila's lips quivered, and she couldn't find the words. After seeing the mayhem that Angie had caused at the table, she knew there was nothing she could say to make things better.

After growing impatient, Angie started shouting. "You don't wanna talk! You always have an opinion! Out with it!"

Aunt Sheila held her head high and sat up as straight as she could. "You need help Angie. We should call your doctor!"

Angie just laughed in her aunt's face. The doctors didn't do anything to help her, and they most certainly couldn't help her now. Even though it made her laugh, she knew that she had to stick with the plan.

Angie rushed outside once again to the garage. After finding a pair of pruning shears that she used seasonally in her garden, she rushed back to the dining room table. Waving the handheld tool in the air, Angie stood next to her aunt and watched as she turned her head trying to ignore her.

"Aaauuuuntttt Shhheeeeellllliiiaaaa!" Angie drug out the name for some added suspense. "Stick out your tongue! I'll make sure you never speak again."

The old woman clinched her false teeth together and pinched her lips tightly together. She looked like a child that was refusing to eat their vegetables. Her squished up, wrinkled face made Angie laugh even harder.

After clanging the cold metal of the pruning shears against her aunt's face, she tried to wiggle the sharp tip of the blade into her aunt's mouth. However, there was just a clanging noise as the metal met her dentures.

Clank. Clank.

Sheila felt the dentures move around her mouth, but still she refused to open her jaw. She intended to keep her tongue.

"Fine. You wanna be that way? I'll give you a choice! It's either your tongue, or Uncle Joe's!" Angie looked towards her old uncle.

Joe was so scared that he wet

his pants and the smell of urine filled the room. Angie's nose wrinkled and tried to figure out where the offending aroma was coming from.

As soon as she realized it was urine, Angie's head snapped towards Uncle Joe.

"Old man! Don't you wear diapers?"

Joe hung his head in shame and embarrassment. No, he usually didn't need diapers, but he usually wasn't ever this scared before.

Realizing that the tape still covered his mouth, Angie used a fingernail to peel back the tape and pulled it away from his mouth, removing some of his white haired mustache with it.

"Ow!" Joe howled in pain. His old and shaky voice was his only line of defense. "Now, wait a minute young lady! I might be old. But this ain't fair. I've been in this family for over forty years. And I've always been good to you. I mind my own business. And Emily." Joe paused as a tear formed in his eye. "I loved that little girl."

Angie thought about Emily for a moment. Just the mention of her daughter's name had an ill affect on her. Once again, her heart broke into a million tiny pieces. The tears in her uncle's eyes really choked her up and she didn't know how to respond.

She knew that she had to regain control of the situation. She couldn't let a kind old man's words deter her from her plan. But her mind kept going back to the previous Christmas and remembering how Joe had bought Emily her beloved art set.

Angie took the crumpled picture from the pocket of her apron and looked at the hand drawn turkey Emily drew in school. It wasn't a masterpiece, but it was the last picture Emily ever drew. Emily loved art, and wanted to be an artist when she grew up. She just never got the chance to grow up.

Angie placed her larger hand over her daughter's outlined smaller hand. She swore she could feel her daughter's presence. Then Joe coughed, snapping her back into reality.

Angie shook her head yes. "You did love her Joe. But I can't leave any witnesses today." Then she remembered young Freddy with his head still passed out on the table. "Maybe I can make an exception. But you can't tell anyone. It would just ruin everything."

The corners of Joe's mouth turned upward. The man was smiling.

UNCLE JOE

In an attempt to raise his hand and show her scout's honor, Joe's feeble arm shook against the tape on his wheelchair. "I won't tell a soul. I promise."

"I know you won't Uncle Joe. I'll see to that."

Joe's smile slowly faded, not sure what she meant. "Please. Not me. Nor Sheila. I can't stand to watch you hurt her. She had good intentions."

"Good intentions?" Angie was once again screaming. "Her intentions didn't change her life, did they? They changed mine. I'll fix you up."

Angie scurried out of the dining room.

Joe didn't know if that was a threat saying that she was gonna fix him up. But since his and his wife's tape was peeled from the mouths they took this brief opportunity to tell each other how much they loved each other.

After many years of marriage, Joe swore that it hurt him worse to see his wife hurt more than anything Angie might do to him. It wasn't but a couple of minutes before Angie returned with her arms full of stuff.

Uncle Joe tried to peek at what Angie was holding, but his eyesight wasn't what it used to be and he couldn't quite tell what he was looking at.

Angie pulled out a spool of thread and started threading a needle. "It pains you to watch Sheila hurt? Then you won't watch!"

Joe's old man voice cracked as he tried to speak. "No, Ang. You don't have to do this." Then the tears fell down his face like rain from a cloud.

Angie pulled the thread all the way through the head of the needle. "Dry those tears Joe. I promise, I will let you live. But now, you have a choice to make. Do you want me to sew your eyes closed or your wife's?"

The old man just shook his head, It was a decision that he didn't want to make. He didn't understand yet why Angie was playing this game. He knew that she had suffered such an incredible loss, but still knew that this was uncalled for. "No. I won't decide."

Sheila looked at her husband and tried to smile, but she was still pinching her mouth closed in fear that Angie would cut her tongue out.

Angie didn't say anything. Instead, she pulled Joe's wheelchair away from the table where she could stand in front of him. The old man closed his eyes as tight as he could.

Joe tried to squirm his head around, but the muscles in his neck were so weak that Angie could easily hold his head still. Since his eyes were closed, he didn't see the needle as it pierced his upper eyelid, but he sure felt it.

Angie's hand was shaking, and found it hard to pierce such a small piece of meat with the needle. But since she was determined, she carried on and also pierced the lower eyelid. After pulling the thread tight, Joe's eyelid began to bunch up.

"See Uncle Joe, when someone finds you, they can remove the thread. Then you'll be able to see again."

Angie continued pushing the needle in full circles sewing his eyelid closed. She might have been new to torturing people, but she was a great housewife and knew how to sew. This was the easiest part of her day.

Joe was screaming in pain, and a tear fell down Sheila's cheek. She hated watching this being done to her husband, but she didn't dare say a word.

Soon, black thread lined both of Uncle Joe's wrinkled eyelids. Skin was wrapped against itself and bunched up to where he couldn't open his eyes.

Blood lined the needle and the black thread was saturated with a crimson color. The blood was also caked into his eyelashes. He didn't think he could stand the pain much longer and he howled in pain, offending Angie's sense of sound.

"Uncle Joe, I'm going easy on you. But I hate a screamer."

She didn't have to say anymore. He stopped making noise and started grinding his dentures instead, trying to ignore the pain.

Soon, Uncle Joe found his courage. "Please, I beg of you. Don't kill my wife. She's all I have."

POOR
SHEILA

Angie respected her uncle's words. If he didn't want his wife dead, maybe she could work with him. All she hated was how her aunt was constantly sticking her nose into Angie's business. She was nothing more than a busybody without a life of her own.

Even though Sheila wouldn't stick her tongue out, she had other things protruding from her face that Angie could work with. Especially that nose that she couldn't keep in her own business.

Without saying a word, Angie

grabbed Aunt Sheila by the chin with one hand, and used the other hand to hold the pruning shears close to her nose. Sheila thought Angie wanted her tongue, so she still sat with her mouth bunched up.

Instead, Angie ran the tool around the insides of Sheila's nostrils. She placed both tips of the scissor's blades in different nostrils, with the blade facing the septum. One second Sheila's nose was fine, the next her septum was cut and pouring blood all over her blouse.

The pain caused Sheila to open her mouth and scream. Angie took the opportunity to stick the pruning shears into her aunt's mouth. Even though it wasn't clasped onto her slimy tongue yet, Angie felt a pang of accomplishment.

Using the small metal part of the pruning shears, Angie pressed her aunt's dentures forwards, forcing the false teeth to fall out of her open mouth. Without her teeth, Sheila looked like any other old woman with a squashed face.

Just for kicks, Angie ran the tool along her aunt's gums. Sheila knew that she was in trouble. After trying to fish around for her aunt's tongue, Angie grew frustrated.

Instead, she positioned the blades around the gums that used to hold her aunt's dentures in place. She started squeezing the blades together.

Since Sheila's lips were closed, Angie couldn't see the damage that she was doing. However, blood started to leak from the corners of her lips, and Angie knew that she was getting something accomplished.

After remembering some of her oldest memories of her aunt, she remembered how she used to chain smoke and blow the smoke directly into Angie's face. "Where's my manners? Aunt Sheila, I bet you want a smoke don't you? Usually I have a strict no smoking policy. But I'll make an exception for you today."

Aunt Sheila had to open her mouth to spit out some of the blood. The taste of it was making her stomach churn. But the thought of a cigarette made her happy. She shook her head yes, hoping this wasn't a trick.

Angie dug around in her aunt's purse, pulled out a cigarette and lit it. She even held it to Sheila's mouth so she could get a drag off it. When she removed it from her aunt's mouth, the filter was soaked with blood.

"I don't have an ashtray. Where should I put my ashes?" Angie knew it was a trick question.

Angie forced the burnt end of the cigarette into her aunt's eye. Even though Sheila closed her eyelid, Angie pressed through the thin skin and burned her way through. When the hot ash met the mucous of Sheila's eyeball, it made a hissing, sizzling sound. It actually made

131

Angie smile.

After extinguishing the smoke in her eyeball, Angie examined the damage. Aunt Sheila's eye looked like a damaged egg. Her pupil was replaced with a hole, and the whites were now red. Angie laughed in her Aunt's face.

Since Sheila was screaming, Uncle Joe kept asking what was happening, since he couldn't see due to his eyelids being sewed closed.

Angie laughed as she spoke. "Not much. I accidentally burned her eye. Oh yeah, I've also snipped her nose and mouth."

Tears found a way to leak through Joe's sewn shut eyes.

Angie was in her groove. Using her pruning shears, she kept snipping around her aunt's nostrils. She ran the tool along the outer edges until her aunt's nose looked like cauliflower, a bleeding cauliflower at that.

Then, Sheila's ears caught her

attention. The snipping (opening and closing) of the pruning shear blades were so loud to Sheila as they slowly approached her ear. Angie didn't quit cutting until there was no cartilage left around her aunt's ears.

It looked funny. The hole was still there, just the external part of the ear was missing. Angie held a flimsy piece of meat in between her fingers. The ear folded easily. She shoved the folded piece of flesh into her aunt's mouth and held it closed.

"Can't chew it without your teeth can you?" Angie let go of her aunt's face and held up her dentures as a joke.

As soon as Sheila spit her ear out, it landed on the white table-cloth in front of her. Angie used both hands to make it look like the dentures were chewing on the ear, making loud chomping noises.

Sheila opened her mouth to speak, but without her teeth, it was hard to understand what she was saying. "Please. No more."

Angie had to try hard to decipher the old woman's words. She was pretty sure she was asking her to stop. Then a timer went off in the kitchen.

After the ding noise, Angie looked at the kitchen door. "It appears that our meal is ready. Let me go gather the food. We can get back to this later."

Aunt Sheila sighed in relief.

THE MEAL

Just like any perfect hostess would do, Angie went into the kitchen to gather the food. Afterall, the meal was the main event. And presentation was everything.

Angie remembered all the years that the holidays were spent at her house. She had done this dozens of times over the years, even though not everyone always showed up.

First, she grabbed the fine china. Each place setting needed only the finest of plates. That was why she and Larry had spent so much money on a set of dishes. They were only used on special occasions, and Angie couldn't think of a more special time.

The guests who were alert watched as Angie threw the smaller plate on top of the larger plate in front of them. The clinking of the glass grated Angie's nerves, but she was in a hurry and wanted to get this over with soon.

After ensuring that each guest had the proper utensils in the proper order, Angie started bringing out the food. First, she carried the turkey in on a large silver platter and set it in the center of the table.

It took several more trips to bring in all the side dishes. She had spared no expense for this meal. There were casseroles, vegetables, and two different types of potatoes.

After she was done setting everything out, it was a beautiful sight to behold. Everything looked so perfect. Once again, Angie was proud of herself.

Last, but not least, she wanted to make sure that her daughter

Emily was remembered. Angie took the drawing of the hand traced turkey and set it on top of her own plate. Even though the food smelled good, Angie didn't have much of an appetite.

Ever since the doctors had put her on anti-depressant medicine and anti-psychotic medicine she didn't eat much anymore. She hated the way the medicines made her feel. They made her groggy, yet she still didn't sleep at night due to crying.

The doctors had told Larry that the medicine was what she needed after the accident. They told him that it would make her better. She knew in her heart that there wasn't a pill that could make her feel better about losing her daughter.

She thought they were the crazy ones, believing medicine would heal the loss of a child.

The perfect hostess looked around her perfectly set table, and looked at all of her guests. It was now time to wake up the sleeping ones, and get everything started. The party had just begun.

Joe and Sheila were the only guests paying any mind to what she was doing. Actually, Joe couldn't watch due to the thread in his eyelids, but Sheila was watching with her bloody nose and missing ear. The blood dripping from her mouth was making a mess all over the white table cloth.

Angie looked at her sister and brother-in-law. She knew that she wanted to wake them. Unfortunately, she knew there was no waking Scott. She had killed him prematurely, and wished she hadn't done that.

Her young nephew, Freddy, was still passed out. Angie walked over to him and pressed her ear to his tiny back. She wanted to ensure that he was still breathing. She would hate herself if she had overdosed him. He was actually innocent in all of this.

As she bent down to press her ear to his back, she hesitated for a split second, afraid that she might not hear any breath moving around in his lungs. Eventually, her ear found its way and heard that he was breathing.

Now, all she had to do was decide whether or not she wanted him awake for this next part. One side of her wanted him awake to witness what she was doing and explain why she was doing it. The other side of her hoped he would sleep through everything to protect his innocence.

Once again, Angie placed her large hand over the smaller tracing of her daughter's hand. She loved the turkey picture her daughter drew for the holidays. It would tell her what to do. She knew Emily was with her, watching her extract revenge on her family. Emily would guide her and help her do what she had to do next.

THE MAIN COURSE

Angie thought about making a loud noise to see if her sister Faith and her brother-in-law Mark were still alive. She hadn't done anything that should have killed them, and hoped they were just passed out from the pain.

But she also knew a loud noise would wake Freddy, so she decided against it. Instead, she took a large fork and took turns poking Faith and Mark in their heads.

Faith was a sight to see. The hot grease that had been poured on her earlier left oozing blisters and redness in her skin. Half of Faith's face wasn't even recognizable as a face.

Mark wasn't pretty to look at either. The hammer had done some pretty serious damage to his face. He would never see out of the eye that Angie struck with the tool.

"Wake up." Angie poked their heads repeatedly.

Eventually, Faith's head started moving, and she slowly opened her eyes and started screaming. She was sitting directly across from Uncle Joe and saw that his eyes were sewn shut. A quick glimpse at Aunt Sheila and her missing ear was revolting. She saw that Sheila's nose looked like it had been turned inside out. Plus, the white milky juice running from her eye was disgusting.

As she turned her head, she saw that Mark was waking up, too. She breathed a sigh of relief. He wasn't dead, even though his face and hands were damaged, probably beyond repair. She could tell by looking that her brother, Scott, was dead.

But thankfully, Freddy appeared to just be sleeping. At least she hoped he was just sleeping. Then, she looked at Angie.

Her sister was covered in blood, but still had a smile plastered to her face. Faith knew she only had one chance to try and make this right and she knew that her family needed her to make this right.

"I am so sorry Angie. Everything you've been through. It's been too much for you. From now on, I'm gonna be a better sister. I promise." Faith lied, hoping she could talk some sense into her sister.

Angie cocked her head towards her sister. "Where were you a month ago?"

Faith didn't know the correct response, so she fudged it. "I know. I will take some of the blame. But I can't change the past. I wish I could, but I can't."

Angie teared up, and the water from her eyes started mixing with the blood on her face. She wanted to believe her sister. She did love her sister. She just felt broken right now, and she wished she could do something to fix herself.

Angie had thought that revenge would make her feel better, but she didn't feel better. It didn't bring Emily back to life. The only logical thing to do was take their lives. She didn't want to speak anymore. She didn't need Faith to try and get in her head like the doctors had tried to do while she was in the mental hospital.

Faith was the first one that she had to eliminate. She had to shut her up. Without saying a word, Angie stood behind her sister and placed her hands on her shoulders. Faith flinched in pain from her burns.

Very slowly, Angie raised the large dinner fork over her head, and forced it into the tender skin of her sister's neck. The not so sharp prongs bit into her skin, but not too deep. Faith howled in pain.

Mark was screaming for Angie to stop. But she didn't. She raised the fork again and stabbed it harder into her sister's neck. However, it still didn't go as deep as Angie wanted it to.

Angie made her way into the kitchen and came back out with a metal meat tenderizer. It looked somewhat like a hammer, but it had large blocks on both ends with jagged indentions in them. She raised the tenderizer over her head, and repeatedly pounded it into her sister's skull.

It took a half a dozen blows, but soon Faith's head slumped forward, and pieces of brain were showing. Her grey matter was splattering all over the white table cloth. Soon, there was no life left in Faith.

Mark was hysterical watching his wife being murdered. Angie

didn't want his screams to wake Freddy, so she grabbed the large knife from the turkey plate. Mark closed his better of the two eyes so he wouldn't see what was coming.

Angie grabbed him by the head of his hair, pulling his head backwards, exposing his neck. She ran the sharp blade across the flesh of his neck, and all at once loads of blood poured free. Mark's last words sounded like gurgling noises.

Aunt Sheila was trying to watch with her good eye. She didn't want to die, so she made sure to not make a noise. Periodically, Joe kept asking what was happening, but Sheila didn't dare answer him.

With a crazed look in her eye, Angie looked at her aunt. "Out of respect for Joe, I'm giving you two choices. Either die, or never speak again. The choice is yours."

Sheila shook her head. "I'll never speak again, I promise."

"Stop!" Angie didn't want to

hear her lies. "Choose now. Death or life?"

Sheila went into shock and sat completely still.

Uncle Joe answered for her. "Please, Ang. Let her live."

Angie walked around the large table, and told her aunt to stick her tongue out, but she wouldn't move. Then Angie had a thought. She had seen plenty of movies. She knew that the vocal cords were in the front of her neck.

However, she was no surgeon, and didn't know exactly where the vocal cords were, but she didn't see any harm in doing an experimental surgery. Angie grabbed a smaller knife and started poking around her aunt's neck. Sheila tried to squirm, but she didn't dare scream.

Angie didn't press too hard as she took the tip of the blade and started digging around the fleshy part of Sheila's neck. Angie didn't want to dig too deep, so she just made several small gashes into the neck.

Small lines of blood poured down into Aunt Sheila's old woman cleavage. Eventually, Angie found something tough to cut into. Maybe it was vocal cords, maybe it was tendon. There was no way to know, but Angie was enjoying it anyhow.

Angie started sawing into the tough insides of Sheila's throat. But then she must have gone too deep, because a steady stream of blood flowed from her aunt's neck. She knew that she had accidentally killed her aunt.

For now, she didn't want to tell Uncle Joe. He could find out later, after she was long gone. She didn't want to hurt his feelings any worse than she already had. Emily loved her Uncle Joe, and Angie respected that.

FREDDY

Uncle Joe kept asking what was happening and Angie told him to be quiet. She told him that Aunt Sheila was just passed out. She hated lying to the old man, but it was the easiest way.

Since she had properly taken care of all of her guests, she was down to Freddy. Her special nephew. She wanted to do this part perfectly.

After wiping her face with a cloth napkin, Angie very gently shook her nephew awake. His little brown eyes started to open, but she could tell that he was still a little sedated.

Freddy kept blinking his eyes,

trying to get them to focus. As he tried to raise his wrists to wipe the sleep from his eyes, he realized that he couldn't move his hands.

"It's okay Freddy. Aunt Angie has a story for you. Do you want to eat first or hear the story first?"

Freddy's eyes still wouldn't open. The medicine was too powerful for him. He just kept blinking. "I'm tired. I wanna sleep." A bit of drool pooled from his lips.

Angie patted her nephew on his head as his eyes closed. "That's okay. How about I tell you a story to go to sleep to?"

Angie saw that he was trying to wipe his eyes. She wanted him to wake up, so she cut his wrists and legs free from the tape. She didn't want to scare the boy any worse. She knew eventually he would see all the dead people around the table.

Freddy rubbed his eyes, but they still wouldn't open. She regretted giving him so much of a sleeping pill.

"A few years ago, my Mommy got sick. Her sister didn't want me to put her in a hospital. And your mommy wouldn't help me take care of her. Do you understand Freddy?"

Freddy just kinda nodded his head while he rubbed his eyes. They still weren't open.

"Do you know what happened to Emily?"

Freddy thought really hard, but his little boy brain wasn't functioning like it usually did. "Mom said she went to heaven."

Angie never knew for her sister to be religious, but still the sentiment made her tear up.

Angie thought back to that day. The day that she had refused to visit in her mind. But she had to come up with a way to explain to Freddy everything that happened.

Approximately One Month Earlier

Larry finally talked Angie into

going to the hair salon and having her hair done. Her mother's dementia had progressed in the recent time, making taking care of her mother even more taxing.

She hadn't been doing anything to take care of herself, and it had taken a toll on her marriage's sex life. Larry admitted to barely even being attracted to her anymore.

Reluctantly, she made an appointment at the salon, under the pretense that Larry would stay home and watch her mother and Emily. When her cell phone rang while she was sitting under a hair dryer, she almost dismissed the call. It was from an unknown number.

But something inside of her told her to answer the phone.

She would have never dreamt that it would be a police officer on the other end of the phone giving her heartbreaking news. When she was informed of the car accident, she assumed her mother must have convinced Emily to go for a car ride with her.

But then that didn't explain where Larry had been.

She didn't remember much about every little detail since she was so devastated and her mind snapped. All she knew were the facts.

Larry left them alone to go to a bar. He was at fault.

Emily's small body was thrown through the windshield, killing her on impact after being cut open by the glass. Her small face was cut to shreds and they had a closed casket funeral. She had been in the driver's seat.

Her mother was always asking people to drive her places, but why would her young daughter drive a car? Did her mother convince Emily to drive? Did she tell her it would be okay?

Even though their car was small, there was no way that Emily could reach the pedals and see to drive.

Even though those details weren't clear, the accident with a large semi truck killed both of them.

Afterwards, Larry had to commit

Angie to a hospital where they kept her sedated. She had been consumed with grief and contemplated suicide. She didn't know how she could go on living after losing her daughter.

She fought away the tears, and proceeded to tell her story.

"I went to get my hair colored. The first time in a couple of years. Larry was supposed to stay home with grandma and Emily." She looked at her dead husband on the floor. "But he went to a bar instead. To watch some game."

Freddy just kinda nodded, trying to fight sleep. The food smelled good, and his stomach growled out of hunger. Angie started putting food on his plate, thinking maybe it would help wake him up.

"Anyways, while I was at the salon, I got a phone call. Telling me there had been an accident." She cut a small piece of turkey for her nephew, and held it to his mouth.

Freddy took the meat and chewed on it, still trying to open his eyes.

"Anyways, grandma's mind didn't work. She thought Emily was somebody else. She convinced her to get in the car and drive her somewhere. You know children aren't supposed to drive, right Freddy?"

Freddy shook his head yes as he chewed on the turkey.

"There was a car accident. That was why we buried grandma and Emily. They both died." Angie froze as she said the words. The painful memories resurfaced and she didn't know how to deal with the pain.

Angie, once again, fought back tears. "That was wrong. It wasn't my fault. It was everyone else's fault. And when you do bad things, you're punished, right?"

Freddy shook his head yes as Angie fed him some more turkey.

"Well, your mommy did bad and I punished her. Just like

everyone else. Do you understand Freddy?"

"Aunt Angie, I'm so thirsty."

Angie poured her nephew a glass of water. He finally opened his eyes to take a drink, his throat was so dry and he was so thirsty. When his eyes opened, he saw all the blood and all the dead bodies.

Angie grabbed his little face. "Look at me, Freddy. Don't look at them. Me and you are going somewhere far away. Me and you will be a family now."

Freddy's young mind couldn't make sense of what he was seeing. "Mommy! Daddy! Wake up!"

Angie grabbed both of his shoulders and shook the young boy. "No Freddy! They're not waking up! It's me and you now!"

FORGOTTEN COUSIN PHIL

Cousin Phil's eyes had started to open. The side of his head was hurting so bad. It was the worst headache he ever had in his life. He tried to feel the side of his head, and realized that his hands and legs were taped to the legs of the table.

He looked around, and saw Larry's dead body lying on the floor. He was trying to remember what happened, but his brain was fuzzy. Then it started coming to him.

He remembered seeing his family tied up to the dining room chairs. Then he thought he remembered Angie hitting him with the bottle of wine. But that didn't make sense. He wondered if he was dreaming.

However, Larry's dead body and the blood soaked into the carpet was proof that he wasn't dreaming. He could hear Freddy crying, and Angie telling him that they were going to live far away.

He knew that Angie had taken Emily and her mother's death really bad, but he had no clue she had gone full crazy.

Even though his head was hurting, he lowered his mouth to the tape that was binding his wrists. He moved slowly and methodically, hoping that Angie wouldn't notice him under the dining room table.

It took a couple of minutes, but eventually, he chewed through the thick tape that was binding his wrists. He moved even slower as he lowered his hands to his legs to undo that tape.

Whenever Angie quit talking, he laid completely still, so as to not draw attention to himself.

Eventually, his hands and feet were free of his bindings, but he didn't know what to do next.

He could see that Freddy was still sitting. Angie was standing beside him. With as bad as his head hurt, he didn't know if he could stand or not and keep his balance. So he laid still, trying to regain his strength and confidence.

He could hear Angie asking Freddy if he wanted some dessert. The boy was still crying, and Angie was doing anything she could to cheer the boy up. Phil watched Angie's feet as she walked into the kitchen to grab the cake.

He knew that he only had one chance. So he laid still, and he waited.

When he saw Angie's feet coming back into the dining room, standing at the head of the table, Phil mustered up every bit of strength that he had. In one swift motion, Phil raised to stand on his feet and grabbed the edge of the dining room table.

Even though he felt dizzy, Phil managed to flip the heavy dining room table. It hit Angie and knocked her sideways. The table landed on its side, and pinned Angie up against the wall.

Phil was so dizzy, he couldn't stand anymore. "Freddy! Grab the knife! Stab Angie!"

A tired Freddy looked around in a daze. He was mad at the world. He was mad at his Aunt Angie because his mommy and daddy wouldn't wake up. Freddy found the knife, and saw his aunt pinned to the wall.

Angie was crying. "No Freddy! Don't make me punish you, too."

Freddy froze not sure what to do. When the table flipped, it turned

Faith's chair sideways. Freddy laid on the floor next to his mom, begging her to wake up.

Angie struggled with the table, and freed herself from it.

Cousin Phil found his footing. "Freddy! Give me the knife."

The boy just laid on the floor, crying with his mother's corpse.

Cousin Phil bent down to take the knife from Freddy's hand. Then he felt the meat tenderizer bash him in his fragile skull.

Angie laughed as she repeatedly bashed her cousin's skull in. Small fragments of bones littered the carpet as blood poured from Phil's head.

The whole time, Uncle Joe kept asking what was happening. Nobody bothered to tell him.

ONE YEAR LATER

As they entered another hotel, the sleepy child wiped the sleep from his eyes. They had been in the car for hours, and car rides always made him sleepy. They had seemed to always get different cars and sleep somewhere different every night.

"Remember, today your name is Toby."

The young boy just shook his head. His name seemed to change everyday, too. It seemed like a long time since someone had called him Freddy.

The child did what his aunt asked of him. He remembered how she punished his parents when they were bad, and he didn't want to be punished in the same way. He did his best to be a good boy.

I hope you enjoyed this story. Find me on Facebook (Sea Caummisar) or on Twitter (@SeaCaummisar). I love hearing from readers! I also have plenty of other stories available on Amazon. Be sure to check them out.

See ya next read

.

Printed in Great Britain
by Amazon

61125183R00099